RED SQUIRREL BOOKS

Published in 2014 in Great Britain by Barrington Stoke Ltd
18 Walker Street, Edinburgh, EH3 7LP

www.redsquirrelbooks.co.uk

This story was first published in a different form in
Read Me a Story, Please, Orion Children's Books, 1998

Text © 1998 Michael Rosen
Illustrations © Chris Mould

A CIP catalogue record for this book is available from the British Library upon request

ISBN 978-1-78112-374-4

Printed in China by Toppan Leefung PTE. Ltd

This book belongs to:

_____

To read with:

_____

WOLF MAN

MICHAEL ROSEN & CHRIS MOULD

RED SQUIRREL BOOKS

People were running down the street screaming.

"Look out! Look out! Wolfman has escaped!"

The people were right.

Wolfman had broken out of his cage and now he was roaring and rampaging around town.

Everyone was rushing to get indoors.

They were very afraid.

Outside, Wolfman was ripping up
paving stones. He was biting into
trees and eating lamp-posts.

It was the most horrible thing ever.

The Prime Minister said, "Send in the army!"

But the army sent back a message. It said,
"Sorry, we can't come. We're too scared."

Things looked bad.

Wolfman was heading down Coppers Road. People were looking out from behind their curtains.

'Please, please, please don't come near our house, Wolfman,' they were thinking.

But Wolfman marched on.

Where was Wolfman going?

To the park? No.

To the swimming pool? No.

The people saw that Wolfman was heading for the house where the Chief of Police lived.

And the Chief of Police was in the back room, hiding behind the armchair.

Wolfman marched on.

Nearer and nearer to the house of the Chief of Police.

Stomp, stomp, stomp.

The ground was shaking.

"Please, please, please go away, Wolfman," the Chief of Police sobbed.

But Wolfman didn't stop.

Wolfman got to the garden gate in front of the Chief of Police's house.

Wham! He kicked it over.

Up the garden path.

"What do you want, Wolfman?" the Chief of Police
called out. "Just say! What do you want?"

There was a moment's silence.

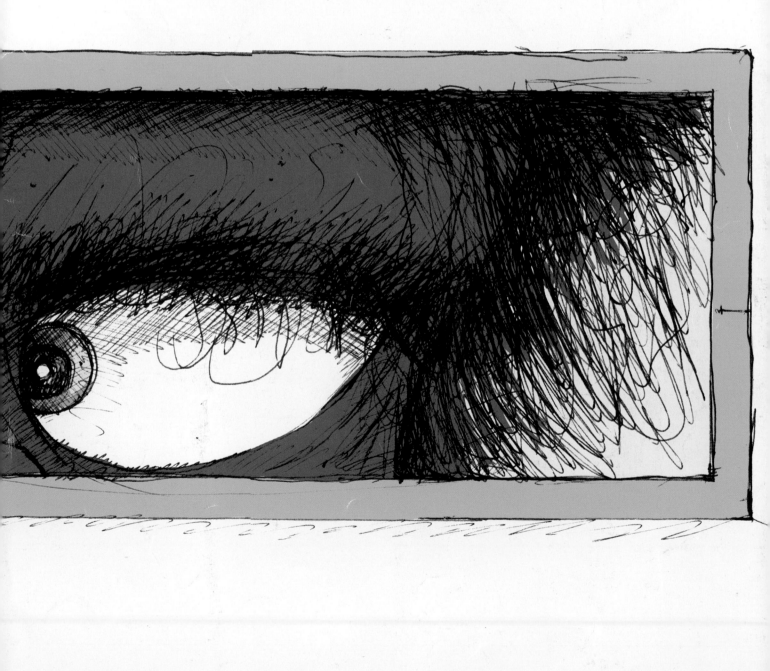

And then, in a little moany voice, Wolfman said, "Can I use your toilet?"

Grow a love of reading

RED SQUIRREL BOOKS